WORK-IN-PROGRESS

10 9 8 7 6 5 4 3 2 1

ISBN 9781020001079

45 Alternate Press, LLC
Hampton, Virginia

WORK-IN-PROGRESS

A NOVELLA

RAN WALKER

PRAISE FOR RAN WALKER

Thank you, Ran, for picking up the guitar of fiction and fretting together characters of such warmth, depth, and humanity.

TYEHIMBA JESS, PULTIZER PRIZE-
WINNING AUTHOR OF OLIO

Walker does an excellent job of pushing the racial envelope [...], confronting preconceptions and notions while always helping readers see the shifting black persona.

SHONDA BUCHANAN, AUTHOR
OF EQUIPOISE: POEMS FROM
GODDESS COUNTRY

Walker's clarity of style and smooth, mellifluous language… place him among the cadre of new black voices budding with fresh, ripe tales of a past and present yet to untold.

DANIEL BLACK, AUTHOR OF
PERFECT PEACE AND LISTEN TO
THE LAMBS

For Sabin,

Something a little different, more FE than LB

NOTE FROM THE AUTHOR

The style and nature of this novella is heavily influenced by the Argentinean writer César Aira's *"fuga hacia adelante"* (flight forward) writing philosophy. This is my humble attempt at paying homage to this creative approach.

"Better the illusions that exalt us than ten thou-
sand truths."
— **Alexander Pushkin**

1

A few years ago I had a number of dreams about flying. I would be standing on the sidewalk that ran across the front of my childhood home. Stepping back so my heels touched the first line in the bumpy concrete, I'd stare out at the endless pattern of squares before of me, this weathered runway of my childhood. Once I was ready, I would run as fast as I could, leaning forward ever so slightly. And like that, my hands extending like I was preparing to do the breast stroke, I would leap forward into the air, swimming through the atmosphere, afraid of rising too high because my fear of heights had not yet abated. I would fly until I got tired, then wake up.

Every dream was a chance to practice my flying a bit more. I was never as good as I should have been, though, and I know this is because I would never allow myself to fly very far above the ground.

In the morning I often found myself more tired than I had been before I went to sleep, suddenly disappointed by my inability to hover even slightly above the plain earth of my small town.

My current terrestrial day job consists of my plodding through the square maze of Tillman's Department store, draped in in a dull brown smock, pulling a stock cart back and forth .

It's the kind of job you work when you need a huge nudge to get off your ass and do something more productive with your life, a job that so ideally encapsulates the mundanity of my town, a place better known for its Clark Kents than its Supermen.

Still, the job pays well enough that I can afford my one-bedroom apartment. I can truly be invisible in a town like this.

This place is not unlike my hometown, where the sparse land seems to vomit forth invisible people. My decision to leave my hometown was the byproduct of the town not being big enough for both my ex and me. There was no safe hour to grocery shop or get gas because my mind had cloned her into all of these places, where occasionally the real person would emerge, her once tender lips twisted into a devious smile, an eternal reminder that she had managed to find love—and therefore happiness

—after I stumbled past her ultimatum for marriage. She married an invisible man, and the last time I saw her, they were working on an invisible child.

I had to leave, though. She was invisible to everyone, except me.

2

This new town is famous for being the hometown of someone famous, and every corner is a
reminder that someone famous once lived here
—and left.

Some days I think about leaving, too, but
then the Holden Caufield in me forces me to
fold.

My footprints here are small, negligible. I
can be and not be at the same time, though I
sometimes feel like someone will discover me
and hoist me from obscurity so that my warts
are laid bare. I'd suddenly be that guy from that
town who once loved that girl whom he still
loves. The auburn in my cheeks will tell the
story.

3

The walls of my apartment are thin, and I can often hear my neighbors making love on the other side of the headboard of my bed. I am tempted to touch myself, but I fear they will hear me, too.

4

My bed has been empty since I arrived. I sleep on the couch in the den. Even though the sheets have been washed a hundred times, I still swear I can smell traces of my ex in them.

I once bought a fresh set of sheets using my employee discount at Tillman's, but upon inhaling their newness, I became convinced my ex had driven over to this new town to purchase and then return them, but not before disrobing and carefully rolling her naked body across every corner of the fabric.

The white noise of my television whispers me to sleep, and I sometimes dream of infomercials that offer lessons on how to fly.

It started with her hands, delicate and soft, worthy of their own Naruda poem. They were holding something or another—that wasn't me—and I longed to be the object of their curiosity.

I knew I would love her, if given the chance. It wasn't that difficult a decision to make—not unlike the ultimatum. Some days I think if she hadn't forced the issue, we'd have grown old together, sipping Arnold Palmers while staring at the sunset from the porch of our dream house.

In Physics force causes a change in the motion of something. Apparently, in relationships it can do the same thing.

Do I still miss her?

Does it matter?

6

A new co-worker at the store has taken to sidling up next to me and telling me the random thoughts in her head. It's a refreshing change, even when she tells me our assistant manager has a voice so deep that it makes her vulva vibrate.

I tell her about the time I caught a guy stealing a box of tampons. She responds by telling me she hopes our assistant manager never hums over the store loudspeaker.

I nod my agreement.

7

My ex kept the TV, and I never bought another one. Instead, I opt to go watch the local bowling league across town. I have a favorite bowler. She averages 205, and I'm hoping her team takes the top spot this year, after coming in second last year.

Oh, the suspense is killing me.

8

I used to spend a lot of time on social media to pass the time. Then one day I read a post and thought to myself that guy really needs to get laid.

I vowed to never write another post like that and deactivated my account.

Living your life online is different from living your life in your head, which is different from living your life.

9

I read a short story today about a guy who loved a huntress but failed to gain her interest. He decided to get a taxidermist to prepare his body for presentation to her. As wild as this idea is, it would have never worked with my ex. According to her, I was already full of stuff.

10

Some days I feel like an incomplete drawing, as if I am a stock character in my own life. I am embarrassed I have allowed myself to dwell in this bubble of melancholy for so long, especially when my own actions served as the catalyst for my current situation.

If life were a plot, I would probably move on and seek out a new hero's journey, doing my best to ignore the fact that my hands feel unsteady, my mouth unconvincing, and my motivation nonexistent. Surely there is a chance for a better *me* out there, somewhere.

11

While stocking store brand toilet paper, I notice my new co-worker friend approaching. She asks if our store discount applies to such items. I reply that it does. She nods and stands there for a moment. She then asks me if I'd like to hang out after work. I nod.

She reaches for my phone, which is riding up my back pocket, and she punches her number into it before sliding it back, slowly, into my pocket, her hand resting there for a moment. She then turns and walks away.

As I stand there, my arms filled with toilet paper, I feel the faint flapping of wings within my stomach, almost ghost-like, attempting to remind me that I actually care about what happens next.

I have never had a woman visit this new apartment. I live in the kind of space only a monk could inhabit. No TV, a shelf full of books largely translated from other languages, and a refrigerator with select items that I hope will shield me from the health ailments that have afflicted my family for generations.

One time when my father was supposed to come visit me, my mother dressed me in pale blue shirt and a clip-on paisley tie. He never arrived that day, though. Instead, he called my mother and asked to speak to me. When my mother handed me the phone, my father told me he had been headed to the car to come pick me up when The Gouch got him.

I remember bursting into tears. I didn't know who or what a Gouch was, but I knew it had my father. I told my mother we had to go and rescue him. Once she was able to stop her laughter long enough to calm me down, she explained to me that my father suffered from an ailment called "gout," that could become debilitating if he consumed too much purine in his diet to knock his uric acid levels out of wack. So not only did my father eat too much of the wrong food, he couldn't even pronounce the name of his affliction.

So my refrigerator's contents are designed to help me avoid high blood pressure, high cholesterol, diabetes (or as Big Mama calls it, "sugar"), and, yes, "the gout." So my apartment, kitchen included, is not set up to impress anyone, let alone my cute co-worker, whose dirty mouth excites me more than I'd care to admit.

She agreed to come by at seven, and once I straighten the handful of items in my den, I sit down with a thin volume of short stories by Fleur Jaeggy and try not to count the minutes.

13

She arrives an hour late, bearing a cheese pizza that neither of us bothers to eat. When she realizes I don't have a TV, she asks me what I do for fun. I point to my Fleur Jaeggy on the coffee table. She shrugs and pulls out her phone.

As if on cue, a persistent thumping sound emanates softly through the apartment. She rises to her feet and follows the sound into my bedroom. I follow behind closely.

She looks at me and asks if they are doing what she thinks they are doing. I nod. She turns on the lamp beside the bed and tells me to kill the overhead lights.

I oblige.

She leans closer to the wall to hear more. She asks me again what I think they are doing, position-wise.

I shrug and say I don't know.

She implores me to use my imagination and

pantomime with her my hypothesis. To encourage me, she lies on her back and invites me to touch her, bend her, flex her into what I imagine is the position of the woman on the other side of the wall.

I am hesitant, but eager. When I wait a beat too long, she insists that she go first and tosses me onto the bed, my back sinking into the comforter. She climbs atop me and says that she thinks the woman is riding the man like this, as she grinds herself into me. Though several layers of clothing separate our flesh, my response to her betrays this.

She stops moving, places a hand against my chest, and pleads for me to tell her my version of the events occurring less than five feet away, through the thin wall that separates the two apartments.

This time I don't hesitate. I flip her onto her back, lift one of her legs over my shoulder, and rest myself against her.

She asks me how hard do I think the guy is.

Pretty hard, I tell her.

She then asks if I am as hard as he.

I shrug and tell her I don't think so.

She asks me what she can do to get me to that point.

I respond that I imagine I would need to be doing whatever *he* is doing, however he is doing it.

She eases from under me and begins to shed her clothes like some svelte, limbed snake and comes to rest on her back, now naked, her shapely leg waiting for my bare shoulder.

I remove my clothes and the light of the lamp casts large shadows of our silhouetted forms against the wall, as we pantomime what we hear, while adding in a few sounds of our own.

14

That night I dream I am flying, my hands parting the air, my feet propelling me forward. I am no higher than the light of the street lamp in front of my childhood home, but I can hear my name being called far above my head, somewhere beyond the clouds.

I find out from glancing at the front page of the local newspaper that my ex's husband has declared his candidacy for state senator. Apparently, my new county falls within his senate district, so I am guessing I will be seeing more of his face—and possibly more of hers as well, if she chooses to hit the campaign trail with him.

They are now visible, but it doesn't matter. I have moved on, I tell myself over and over again.

I have been at work for two hours before my new friend arrives. She eases past me in an empty, but wide aisle. Her initial thought process, I'm guessing, is to come near me to brush her hand across my crotch before heading to get her brown smock out the back of the store. Instead, she grabs hold of my entire package and gently rocks it back and forth before heading to the back. I avoid glancing at the security camera in the smoky bubble overhead. There is no point in giving anyone visual proof of my guilt.

I can still feel her firm grip as I walk toward the front of the store. I can't help but think that she was letting me know she has marked her territory.

My shift goes by slowly, punctuated by occasional glances from my new friend. Before my shift ends, she approaches me to see if I have plans for the evening. I tell her no. Actually, I never have plans, but I don't feel the need to disclose this yet. She asks if she can come over and listen to my neighbors again, the nightly syndicated show that they are.

I tell her yes.

The news of my ex's husband is still ringing in the back of my head, but it is soon overtaken by memories of my new friend's body frozen beneath me, as if in *flagrante delicto*, concealed on the edge of midnight, our secrets threatening to burst forth into the light.

This new town does not have a mall, a movie theater, or a decent restaurant that is not a part of some chain, but it *does* have an amazing indie bookstore, so all is forgiven.

In the window between my shift ending and the sequel to the previous night's escapades, I cocoon myself in the back corner of the store with a novella by the Argentinean writer César Aira. This is the fourth book I have picked up by him. In many ways his "fuga hacia adelante" style of writing is reflective of my own life, in that each day is often a random leap forward that has little, if anything, to do with the events of the previous day. For the satisfaction my co-worker gives me, she could just as easily poison my ice cream and I wouldn't be surprised.

Truth be told, it's not so much that my life is random; it's just that I've lost the interest in finding the common denominator that connects the days.

I buy the book and take it home, where I can savor the remaining moments of my solitude.

Across the street from my apartment is a park, and in that park is the statue of a famous person I have never heard of. From the dates on the plaque below his feet, it is clear those who knew him best have long since passed away. Someone in this town apparently—at some point in the past—refused to let this person be forgotten.

I doubt there will ever be a statue of me anywhere, and I am content with that. There are more than enough monuments in the world already.

Maybe I will write a book one day and have that serve as my testament to the fact that I was here. Most writers are invisible, but their books are not.

That is the way it should be.

My co-worker arrives early. This time instead of pizzas she has brought toys.

We make small talk for a few minutes. Then she takes out a pocket rocket and sets it to "Barry White" mode. I watch her eagerly until she invites me to join in.

My neighbors are curiously quiet. I imagine them pantomiming our movements, the woman holding her husband by his ears as she rotates his head like a spotlight aimed at center stage. By the time I enter her, I am harder than Advanced Calculus.

She talks shit as if the neighbors are listening, and when we hear the rhythmic banging of a headboard through the wall, we smile. For the next hour we engage in this duet, our syncopated melodies fueling the other until the screams of our climaxes become a singular note.

This time my co-worker decides to spend the

night, mainly because she has plans to wake up the neighbors in the middle of the night with our activities.

I decide to get a bottle of water and nap during the meantime.

21

In the middle of the night, we wake up the neighbors.

22

Later, they wake us up in return.

I am sore and tired by the time I make it to work. My co-worker has a later shift and has the luxury of sleeping in.

Tonight I want to be alone—to clear my thoughts—but I know I will cave in. My co-worker has now become my friend, and if she calls later, I will acquiesce, but I am starting to see how my contentment with being alone has begun to evolve into a fear of loneliness, an emotion which had been lying dormant before her arrival.

When I make it home, I am compelled to write a story—no, a book! The idea locks into my head the way that one discerns the exact placement of a puzzle piece. The story will be about a guy who wants to write a formless novella, reflecting the influences of authors whose translations he has read. He will wrestle with a meandering storyline, packed with allusions to reach a place of artistic freedom.

In this novella he will write about a character whose name is never revealed, who is surrounded by people whose names aren't revealed either, a distant take on the invisibility Ralph Ellison describes in his classic novel.

The character would be free falling through life after a relationship melts the wax in his wings. He will attempt to fight the apathy of plunging into the abyss by engaging in sexual encounters with a libertine who works at his job.

It is either meta or autobiographical or both or neither. I drive right in, expecting to have my work interrupted by a call from my friend, a call that never comes.

I write over five thousands words before I fall asleep.

In my dream I am running as fast as I can, trying to take off into the air, but I can't. The air feels too thin to support me, so I keep running until I wake up.

In today's mail I receive a flyer bearing my ex's face. She glows like the trophy wife that she is, her visible baby nestled against her breast, with the candidate's arm wrapped comfortably around her shoulder. She looks even less like the woman I knew, her jeans replaced with a safe suit, her lipstick rich and foreign, far from the fruit-scented lip gloss she used to wear.

I wonder if she is happy with this new costume, this new role she is playing. This new character has never made love in a car or across a dining room table or screamed in a climax loud enough for the neighbors to hear, I imagine. This new character makes love only after carefully bathing and only on the crisp, pristine sheets of her bed, exhaling whispers of satisfaction that would not wake the lightest of sleepers.

I don't recognize her anymore, and when I

realize that she is *gone*, my heart breaks again, this time with no hope of mending.

27

My book wanders forward, the momentum slip-
ping each day I sit down to write. My muse is
gone. It feels as though she is dead and her body
has been laid to rest in some unknown location.
I write a few words, then quickly delete them. I
force myself to put down a few more words and
close my laptop quickly, lest I erase those, too.

I lie in bed staring at the ceiling, listening to Lenny Kravitz's *5* album. At times I want to jump up and down on my bed and rock my face off completely. Other times, I just want to lie there and let the music swirl above me in some ethereal space that I am not occupying.

A knock at the door draws me back into the moment. I walk to the door and gaze through the peephole.

My friend has arrived unannounced and cloaked in a trench coat, reminiscent of the scene in Eddie Murphy's *Boomerang*. I open the door.

She asks if I am alone—a strange question, given that I have allowed her into my apartment. I tell her that I am. She then tells me that she has come to fuck my brains out so that the zombies can't come for me. I ponder this statement but am quickly interrupted when she opens her coat and reveals her nude body, toned and hungry, her pose further enhanced by the pumps she has worn to accentuate the effect of her outfit.

We don't make it to the bedroom, yet later, in our post-coital bliss, I imagine that I can hear the applause of my neighbors next door.

Lying beneath the ceiling fan in my room, I ask my friend what it is that we are doing.

She tells me that we are exploring each other.

I know nothing about you, I tell her, and she shakes her head to challenge me. I suggest that we might actually go somewhere together and do something more traditional, like a date.

She shrugs and asks if I am wanting something monogamous to exist between us. I reply that I have no way of knowing unless we do more than we are currently doing.

She asks me what I enjoy doing. I tell her reading, watching movies, things like that. She tells me that she enjoys having sex.

We look at each other for a moment, and then we go at it again—and again.

Our first "date" involves us driving around in the ritzier part of town, imagining that we live in this house or that house. As soon as the sun sets, we park on the street in front of one of these massive antebellum homes and let our seats back.

She tells me that she wants me to fuck her like the house in the background is hers. I glance at the house and then undress her a bit more slowly this time. I kiss her repeatedly before I enter her.

This time it's different.

Once we finish she holds me in her arms just a little longer. For a minute she does not speak; she only stares at me, as if she sees something she has never really noticed.

I no longer sleep on the sofa, even when I am alone. I swim in my bed, sometimes alone, sometimes buoyed by my friend.

The scent of my sheets is, quite simply, us. I cloak myself in what's left of our union, the sweaty funk of vigorous sex and the subtle traces of our pre-coital fragrances.

It's warm beneath the sheets.

I cocoon myself there, a swollen pupa, waiting to emerge as someone new.

32

When I arrive home from work one day, I see a folded sheet of paper inserted into the groove of my door frame. It's a get-out-the-vote flyer from my ex's husband. I take it inside.

As I sit at the small dining table in my kitchen, I stare at his face. We look nothing alike, his darker, heavier frame, crisp suit, cuff links. We are total opposites. I question how my ex could have ever loved me, when I have absolutely nothing in common with her husband.

Our lives would have been very different. But different how? Would I have still worked at Tillman's? Would I have aspired to more? Would I have held her back from her true potential?

What would our children have been like?

A bystander gazing upon her husband, and then me, would say that my ex dodged a bullet.

She may have.

But I have to believe that what we had was not the worst thing that could have happened to her. After all, love is a good thing, isn't it?

33

Apropos of nothing, I tell my friend about my dreams of flying. She tells me she dreams about flying, too. I ask her what she thinks it means. She tells me that she thinks it might mean that we are rising above the things that hold us down.

I like her answer, but I don't know what it means.

In the darkness of my bedroom, we stare at the ceiling. It seems like it stretches on forever, like a starless night sky.

34

An aisle at a department store seems like it contains an unlimited amount of stuff, but it doesn't. Part of my job is to count and stock every item. A job like this reinforces the idea that maybe everything *is* finite, although it appears infinite. We could probably count just about everything, but the idea that things can be somehow unquantifiable, seems almost divine. So we stop counting, content to stop exploring.

I stare at a giant package of toilet paper and wonder if this is what a mile of it looks like rolled up. If I were to open all of the stock in the store and unroll every single sheet of toilet paper, stretching those sheets into a single line going up into the sky, how close to space would I get?

Then I shake my head. If I were to unfurl a single roll and shoot it into the sky, I would never be able to fly that high.

My friend sees me standing there, staring at the shelves, and walks up to me.

She tells me she has something special for me tonight, but that I have to trust her first.

I tell her that I *do* trust her, and she smiles.

She walks away, and I return to stocking the shelves.

She arrives just before midnight. We head to my bedroom, and she tells me to undress and lie down on my back.

I do as she requests.

She undresses and lies down next to me, the warmth of her body familiar and relaxing.

She tells me to close my eyes. She adds that whatever I do, I must keep them closed.

I nod, squeezing together my eyelids until I see a small burst of color.

She then caresses my chest, gently moving her smooth leg up and down my body until I am erect. She climbs on top of me and pulls our bodies tightly together until we become one.

She moves up and down, swallowing and releasing me with her flesh, and I keep my eyes sealed, even in the darkness of the room.

As she rotates and slides on/over/around me, I feel my body beginning to rise—*our* bodies beginning to rise. She pulls herself closer to me and grinds me with a passion unrivaled by any of my previous lovers, my ex included.

Then I feel the cool air of the room against my back as we lift up from the sheets. We are rising into the air, and my heart begins to race.

I tell myself that I am imagining this, that the sex is so good my mind is playing tricks on me, but a part of me knows I am trying to rationalize what is really happening.

And we keep rising.

My bed is starting to feel hundreds of feet beneath me, and this scares me. Sensing my apprehension, my lover leans close to my ear and whispers for me not to open my eyes.

And we continue lifting up, up, up to a place that feels far beyond the boundaries of my apartment.

She tells me that she wants me to cum with her, and I want to, but I am too afraid. We are too high up.

My legs are now weak, my stomach tight, my erection straining to hold on.

I tell her we are up too high.

She responds that we are not up high enough.

And we lift again.

My heart racing, kicking through my chest, I can no longer take it. If this is an illusion, I have to know. If it is real, I have to know.

I open my eyes.

In the darkness, I can make out her face, barely, and when I can, it seems to oscillate back and forth between her face and the face of my ex.

I told you to keep your eyes closed, she screams at me, releasing me.

And I fall,

fall,

fall,

the air whipping past my face, my naked body, my skin pulled by the wind, as I tumble through the night sky. I try to fly, my arms making swimming motions, the movements I have been practicing in my dreams for years.

And still I fall.

I cannot fly. My arms go still and I look up, where I see my lover hovering in the distance above me. The ground is racing up toward me, so I brace for impact.

Then everything goes white.

I blink my eyes and am blinded by the whiteness before me. It extends in every direction, its snowy, smooth perfection completely untainted. I have no idea which direction I should go in, the whiteness not offering any guidance. So I stand still, surveying all that is around me, my mind racing in place, the reflection of the light on the whiteness still shocking my vision.

From nowhere a shadow swaths the whiteness out ahead of me, and I finally look up. That's when I see His face.

He is staring at me, His face fixed in uncertainty. The massive cannon in His hand sweeps back and forth rapidly far above my head.

I don't say anything. I just stare. I am not afraid, only confused. I wonder what He wants me to do.

We both wait.

He tells me that He started to have me jump

into the body of another character, maybe the ex's husband, but decided against it. He then admits He doesn't know what He wants to do with me.

I tell Him that I was content writing my book and making love to my friend, but when I gaze out at the endless white before me, I realize that the book is gone, my apartment is gone, my ex is gone, and my friend is gone. And it hurts. After all, why should I suffer because the Author has stalled in his creativity.

We stare at each other a bit longer, and I am hoping that His seeing me against this background is giving Him the need to do something with me, but nothing happens.

He is going to make me plead with Him, I see. But I am not too proud for this. I am doing what is necessary.

"Please let me go home," I say.

For a moment He stares at me, and I wonder if He has even heard me. Then, out of nowhere, He smiles and lowers his pen over me.

As the whiteness gives way around me, my room begins to reappear. I am in bed, my clothes draped over the chair at my desk. Nestled in the crevice of my body, my friend yawns and adjusts the placement of her head on my chest.

She tells me that she thought she had lost me when I fell.

I admit the same, but promise her I will listen to her next time and keep my eyes closed.

She nods but adds that I should still work on my flying.

We stare up at the dimly lit ceiling, my blinds cracked to let in the faint glow from the street lights in front of my apartment complex.

I know the ceiling is not there. Maybe even my friend is not there. But somehow *I* am, and I have to believe that everything around me is something other than words painted on paper.

Here I can start over.

Here I can recreate who I am.

Here I can fall in love again.

And here I can begin to give myself permission to fly as high as I want.

fin

ALSO BY RAN WALKER

B-Sides and Remixes

30 Love: A Novel

Mojo's Guitar: A Novel / (Il était une fois Morris Jones)

Afro Nerd in Love: A Novella

The Keys of My Soul: A Novel

The Race of Races: A Novel

The Illest: A Novella

Bessie, Bop, or Bach: Collected Stories

Four Floors (with Sabin Prentis)

Black Hand Side: Stories

White Pages: A Novel

She Lives in My Lap

Reverb

Work-In-Progress

Daykeeper

Most of My Heroes Don't Appear On No Stamps

Portable Black Magic

ABOUT THE AUTHOR

Ran Walker is the author of seventeen books. He has written novels, novellas, short stories, flash fiction, microfiction, and poetry. His short stories, flash fiction, microfiction, and poetry have appeared in a variety of anthologies and journals. Prior to becoming a writer and educator, he worked in magazine publishing and practiced law in Mississippi.

He is the winner of the 2019 National Indie Author of the Year Award (selected by judges from *Library Journal*, *Publisher's Weekly*, Ingram-Spark, St. Martin's Press, and *Writer's Digest*), the 2019 Black Caucus of the American Library Association Best Fiction Ebook Award, and the 2018 Virginia Indie Author Project Award for Adult Fiction. He is also the recipient of both a 2005 Mississippi Arts Commission/NEA artist grant and a 2006 artist mini-grant. He served as an Artist-in-Residence with the Mississippi Arts Commission in 2006. Additionally, he is a past participant in the Hurston-Wright Writers Week Workshop and is the recipient of a fellowship from the Callaloo Writers Workshop.

His novel *Mojo's Guitar* was translated by

renowned French translator Philippe Loubat-Delranc and published in April 2015 by Éditions Autrement as *Il était une fois Morris Jones*. The novel was recently republished in May of 2019 as a part of Éditions Autrement's "Les Grands Romans" collection.

His first collection of poetry, *Most of My Heroes Don't Appear On No Stamps: Kwansabas*, will be published in August of 2019 by The University of Hell Press, based out of Portland, Oregon.

Ran is a graduate of Morehouse College (BA in English), Pace University (MS in Publishing), and George Washington University Law School (JD). He also has a Certificate in Publishing from New York University and has done graduate work in English at Mississippi State University.

Ran is an Assistant Professor of English and Creative Writing at Hampton University and lives in Virginia with his wife and much better half, Lauren, and his amazing little rockstar daughter, Zoë.